FUN FACT FILE: FOUNDING FATHERS

20 FUN FACTS ABOUT AARON BURR

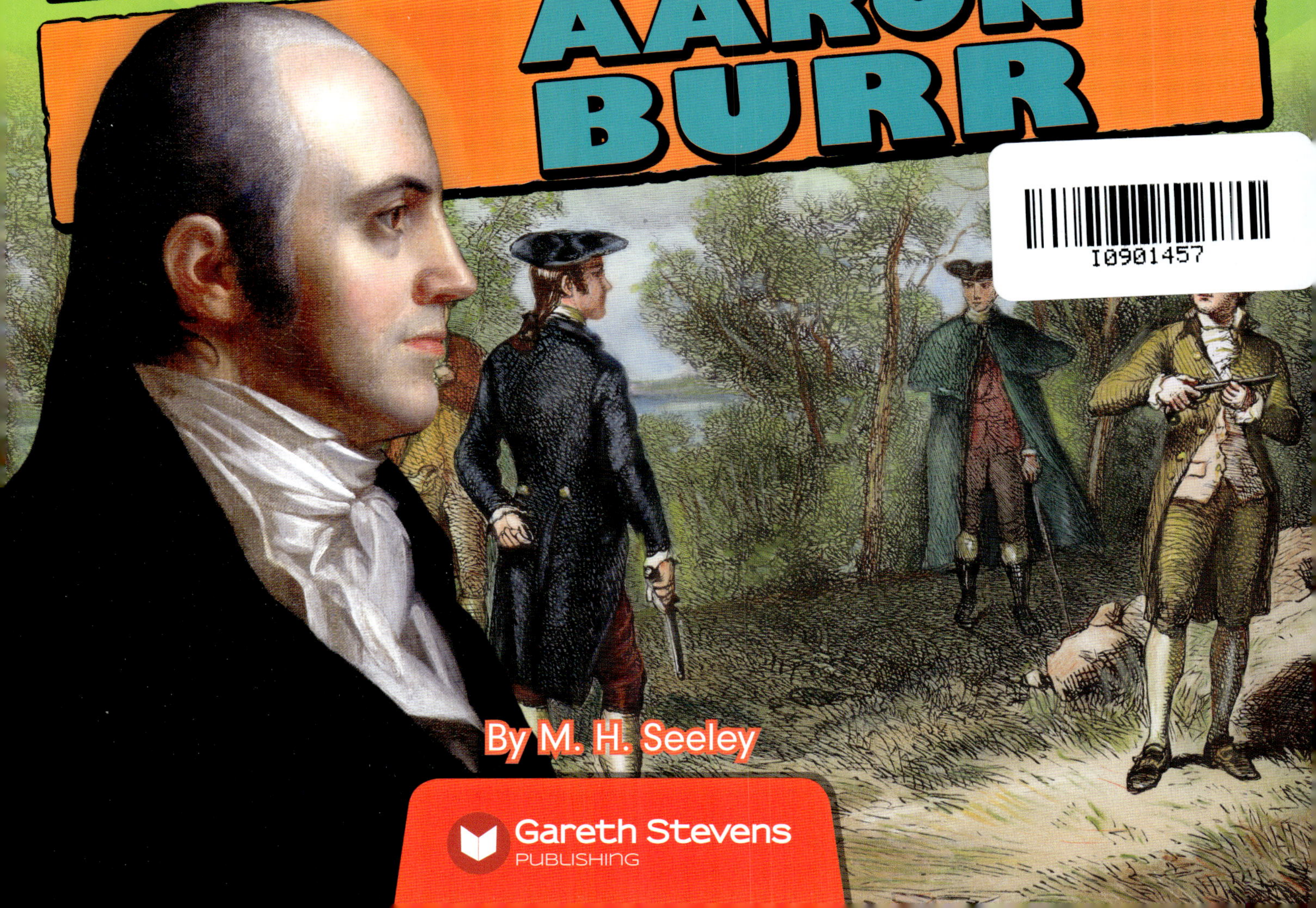

By M. H. Seeley

Gareth Stevens PUBLISHING

Please visit our website, www.garethstevens.com. For a free color catalog of all our high-quality books, call toll free 1-800-542-2595 or fax 1-877-542-2596.

Library of Congress Cataloging-in-Publication Data
Names: Seeley, M. H., author.
Title: 20 fun facts about Aaron Burr / MH Seeley.
Other titles: Twenty fun facts about Aaron Burr
Description: New York : Gareth Stevens Publishing, [2018] | Series: Fun fact file : founding fathers | Includes index.
Identifiers: LCCN 2016056278| ISBN 9781538202876 (pbk. book) | ISBN 9781538202692 (6 pack) | ISBN 9781538202814 (library bound book)
Subjects: LCSH: Burr, Aaron, 1756-1836–Juvenile literature. | Statesmen–United States–Biography–Juvenile literature. | Vice-Presidents–United States–Biography–Juvenile literature. | Burr-Hamilton Duel, Weehawken, N.J., 1804–Juvenile literature.
Classification: LCC E302.6.B9 S44 2018 | DDC 973.4/6092 [B] –dc23
LC record available at https://lccn.loc.gov/2016056278

First Edition

Published in 2018 by
Gareth Stevens Publishing
111 East 14th Street, Suite 349
New York, NY 10003

Designer: Sam DeMartin
Editor: Ryan Nagelhout

Photo credits: Cover, pp. 1 (background), 13 Bettmann/Bettmann/Getty Images; cover (foreground), pp. 1 (foreground), 29 Janneman/Wikimedia Commons; p. 5 Everett Historical/Shutterstock.com; p. 6 EQRoy/Shutterstock.com; p. 7 Bob Burkhardt/Wikimedia Commons; p. 8 Night Gyr/Wikimedia Commons; p. 9 Memtgs/Wikimedia Commons; pp. 10, 16 Futurist110/Wikimedia Commons; p. 11 bobby20/Shutterstock.com; p. 12 Yann/Wikimedia Commons; p. 14 SteinsplitterBot/Wikimedia Commons; p. 15 Ken Wolter/Shutterstock.com; p. 17 chrupka/Shutterstock.com; pp. 18, 20 Billy Hathorn/Wikimedia Commons; p. 19 Fæ/Wikimedia Commons; p. 21 Tupungato/Shutterstock.com; p. 22 Jose Gil/Shutterstock.com; p. 23 zimmytws/Shutterstock.com; p. 24 Kaldari/Wikimedia Commons; p. 25 SuperStock/Getty Images; p. 26 MPI/Archive Photos/Getty Images.

Printed in China

CPSIA compliance information: Batch #CS17GS: For further information contact Gareth Stevens, New York, New York at 1-800-542-2595.

Contents

Words in the glossary appear in **bold** type the first time they are used in the text.

Aaron Burr, Sir

Aaron Burr was born on February 6, 1756, in Newark, New Jersey. His life had a hard start: his parents and grandparents all died when he was a baby. But Burr didn't let this keep him from success. He studied law and became one of America's Founding Fathers. He also killed Alexander Hamilton and may have been a **traitor**.

Many historians haven't known what to make of Aaron Burr. Was he a good man, a bad one, or somewhere in between? You'll have to decide for yourself!

Aaron Burr was many things in his life, including a lawyer, politician, soldier, father, fighter, and maybe a traitor.

Burr's Big Brain

FACT 1

Aaron Burr graduated from the College of New Jersey at just 16 years old!

Burr first applied to the college—which later became Princeton—when he was only 11. But he wasn't accepted until he was 13. He graduated with highest honors in just 3 years. He later studied first religion, then law.

Aaron Burr Hall at Princeton University was named for Aaron Burr's father—Aaron Burr Sr.—who was its second president.

Princeton is one of the oldest schools in the country. It was founded in 1746 and renamed in 1896!

FACT 2

Burr's nickname at college was "Little Burr."

Because he was so young, Burr's classmates called him "Little Burr" while he was at Princeton. He was known to be funny and playful and could get away with things that other students wouldn't dare try—like joining two school groups that hated each other!

FACT 3

Burr once went undercover as a priest.

One of Burr's first military jobs was to help Generals Richard Montgomery and Benedict Arnold start an attack in Quebec, Canada, in 1775. Burr dressed himself as a priest to travel 120 miles (193 km) through British lines to notify Montgomery of Arnold's arrival.

Benedict Arnold

Benedict Arnold is one of the most famous traitors in American history—but when Burr worked with him, he was a well-respected general.

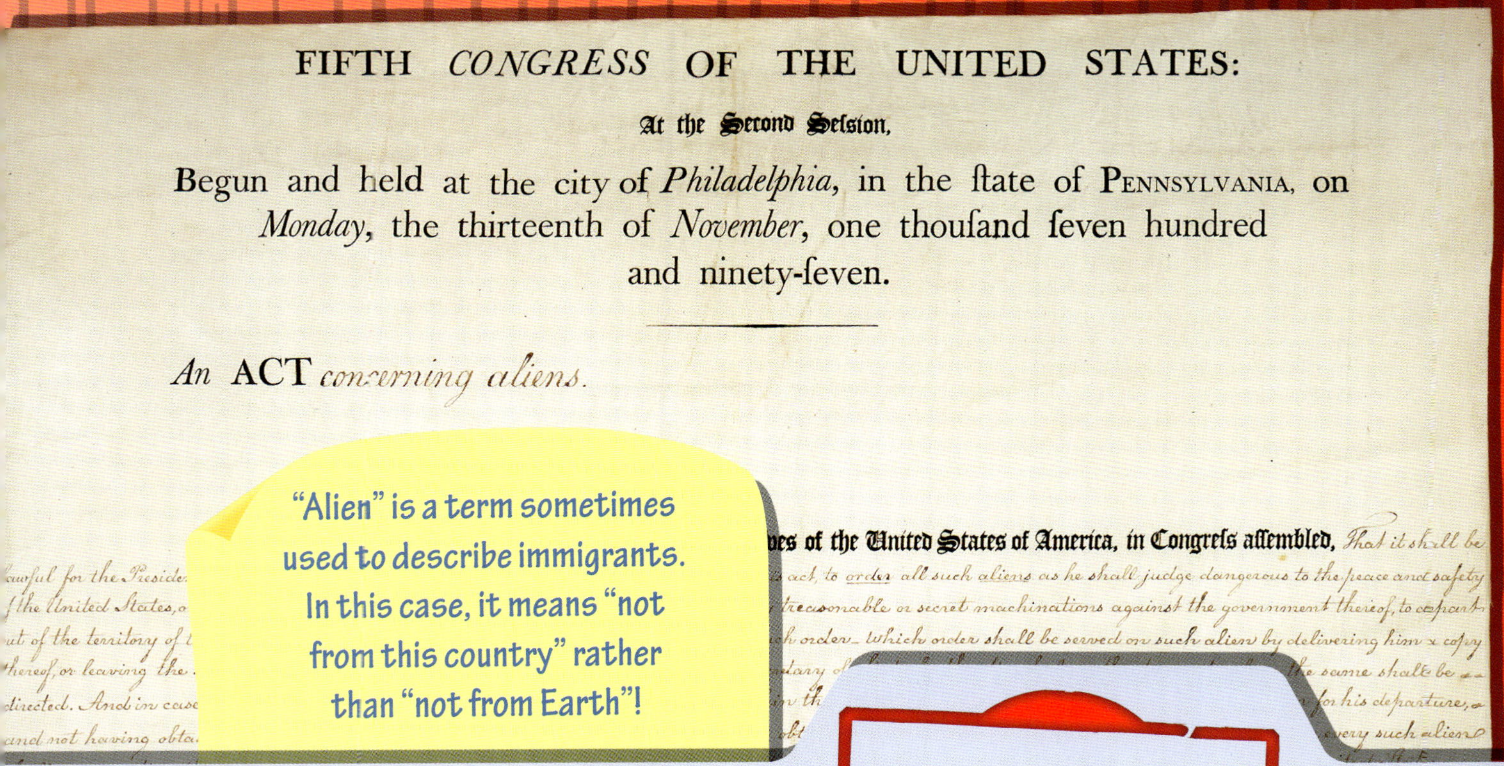
FIFTH *CONGRESS* OF THE UNITED STATES:

At the Second Seſsion,

Begun and held at the city of *Philadelphia*, in the ſtate of PENNSYLVANIA, on *Monday*, the thirteenth of *November*, one thouſand ſeven hundred and ninety-ſeven.

An ACT *concerning aliens.*

...ves of the United States of America, in Congreſs aſſembled, *That it shall be*

"Alien" is a term sometimes used to describe immigrants. In this case, it means "not from this country" rather than "not from Earth"!

FACT 4

Burr fought for the rights of immigrants.

Burr didn't like laws that made it harder for immigrants to vote or gave the government more power to **deport** them. Burr's work against these laws helped earn him the respect of New York's large immigrant community.

FACT 5

George Washington and Aaron Burr didn't like one another.

Burr served as Washington's **aide** for a short time, and both men had lots of respect for one another. But by many accounts, they didn't get along. Washington didn't like Burr's ambition. He thought Burr was "brave and able," but also suspected he was untrustworthy.

Washington respected Burr, but he may not have liked him.

Burr helped lead an attack against forces in Quebec, which today is a French-speaking part of Canada.

FACT 6

Burr risked his life to bring a US general home.

When cannon fire killed General Montgomery during battle in Quebec, Canada, Burr is said to have risked his life trying to rescue the body from the battlefield. But Washington never gave him any honors or medals for it!

FACT 7

Abraham Lincoln

Burr believed that slavery was evil and should be ended right away.

Burr was an abolitionist, or someone who was in favor of ending slavery. In 1785, when he was a member of New York's lawmaking body, it was considering a bill to end slavery slowly. Burr **proposed** instead to end slavery immediately.

Slavery wasn't ended in the United States until 1865 when Abraham Lincoln was president.

FACT 8

Burr found ways around the law to help the people for whom he worked.

In Burr's state of New York, only "**qualified**" voters, or white male property owners, could vote in certain elections. Burr helped people join together in groups so they could afford to buy a piece of land. Everyone who put money toward the land became a "qualified" voter.

In Burr's day, only men could vote—and not even all men!

Bank on It

FACT 9

Burr secretly created what became America's third bank.

New York City had two big problems in Burr's time: dirty drinking water and banks that would only lend to certain people. To help fix both, Burr created the Manhattan Company. It was supposed to clean up Manhattan's water!

Burr's Manhattan Company had a **charter** that allowed the company to use its money like a bank: buying stocks and lending money to its members.

FACT 10

Burr's new bank lent him $60,000!

Before the Manhattan Company, banks were used only by the very wealthy. The Manhattan Company sold shares, or pieces of ownership, for just $50, allowing less wealthy businessmen to take part. But the bank made big loans, too—including loans to Burr himself that totaled $60,000!

Burr's bank was so successful that it's still around today—but you might know it by its new name: JPMorgan Chase.

And the Winner Is...

FACT 11

Burr and Thomas Jefferson tied for president—35 times!

During the presidential election of 1800, Jefferson and Burr tied in the **Electoral College**. The vote was sent to the **House of Representatives**, where they tied again. It took 36 votes before Jefferson became president and Burr vice president!

Thomas Jefferson

In Burr's time, the person who finished second in the Electoral College became the vice president!

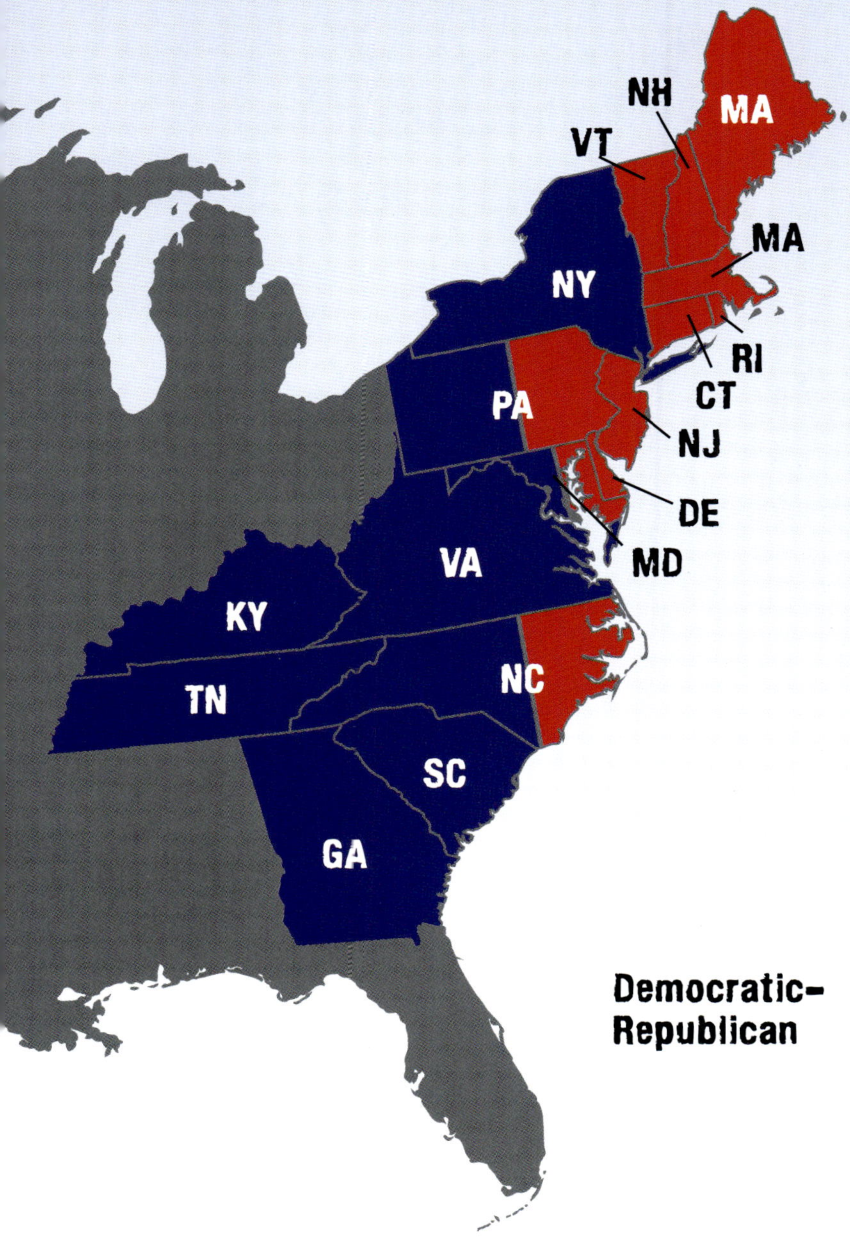

Election of 1800

Candidate and Party	Electoral Votes
Thomas Jefferson Democratic-Republican	73
Aaron Burr Democratic-Republican	73
John Adams Federalist	65
Charles C. Pinckney Federalist	64
John Jay Federalist	1

% Electoral Vote

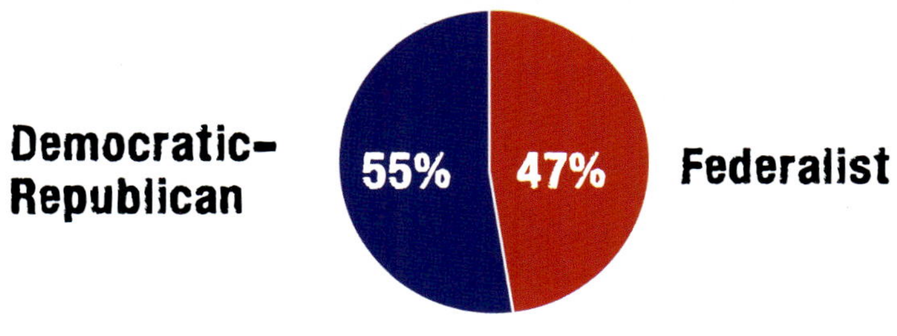

Honor over All

FACT 12

Burr took part in one of the most famous duels in American history.

Burr is probably best known for dueling with Alexander Hamilton in Weehawken, New Jersey. Burr shot and killed Hamilton in 1804. Burr was vice president at the time, but he never again held public office.

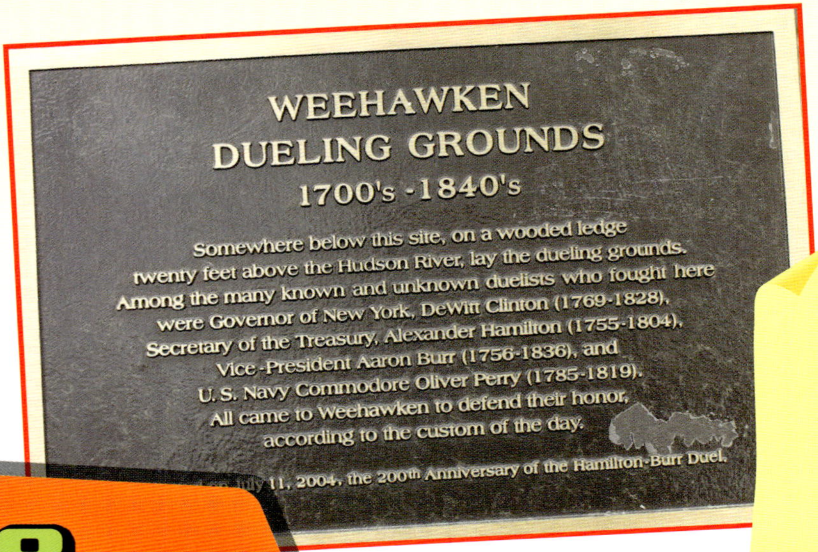

The Hamilton-Burr Duel is one of the most famous events in United States political history. The two dueled over a series of disagreements they had and because Hamilton didn't support Burr in the election of 1800.

FACT 13

Burr had dueled with the brother of Hamilton's wife years before he shot and killed Hamilton.

After Burr created the Manhattan Company, he heard that Hamilton's brother-in-law, John Barker Church, had **accused** him of using the company's money for himself. The two men met in New Jersey, and each fired one shot before Church said he was sorry.

Honor duels happened when someone wouldn't say they were sorry for harming another person's honor, either by saying something about that person or doing something to them.

I Fought the Law

FACT 14

Because Burr had followed the rules of an honor duel, he never stood trial for Hamilton's death.

Burr may have been a killer to the public, but he wasn't a murderer. Though New York and New Jersey both charged him as one, he never went to court. In fact, Burr continued to act as vice president.

Dueling was illegal in most states by the time Hamilton and Burr met on the shores of Weehawken, New Jersey.

FACT 15

When Burr ended his vice presidency, he gave a speech that made the Senate cry!

Burr wanted to go out with a bang when he left office, and he certainly managed it. Burr spoke so beautifully that, according to a senator who was there, when he concluded, a "silent weeping filled the Senate chamber [room] for perhaps five minutes."

US Capitol Building

One of the vice president's duties is to be the president of the Senate.

The Burr Conspiracy

FACT 16

Burr was once accused of trying to start his own country.

In 1807, Burr was arrested in Louisiana Territory for a plan to separate the western US territories from the rest of the nation in order to form a new country under his leadership. He was found innocent, but it's impossible to know what really happened.

The Louisiana Purchase cost $15 million and nearly doubled the size of the United States.

FACT 17

Burr escaped jail time through a hole in the law—a loophole.

Almost everyone agreed that Burr had *tried* to commit treason, or overthrow the US government, in the western territories. But because Burr merely *planned* to act and never actually acted to create the new country, he was found innocent.

The US Constitution defines treason a certain way, so Burr narrowly avoided going to prison.

FACT 18

Burr's first wife, Theodosia Prevost, was the great love of his life.

In an age when many women didn't receive an education, Prevost and Burr's letters to each other read like university **debates**. She was smart and well read. After she died, Burr called her "the best woman and finest lady I have ever known."

Mary Wollstonecraft

Burr had great respect for women's rights. He hung a picture of Mary Wollstonecraft, an early women's rights activist, in his home.

FACT 19

Burr's daughter, also named Theodosia, was very smart and disappeared at sea!

Burr's daughter Theodosia was brilliant, beautiful, and well educated. She might even be the first woman in America to have a college-level education. In 1813, she boarded a ship named the *Patriot* to visit her father. Neither she nor the *Patriot* was ever seen or heard from again!

Theodosia Burr

Theodosia Burr Alston married Joseph Alston in December 1812 and became First Lady of South Carolina before she was lost at sea.

FACT 20

Burr left America for Europe and couldn't come back!

Burr ran off to Europe in 1808 after he was found not guilty of treason. He owed people in the United States money, and many were angry about his treasonous plan. Burr left without a passport, though, and couldn't get back into the United States for years!

Burr's daughter wrote many letters to people in government trying to get her father back from his **exile** in Europe.

Timeline of Burr's Life

1756 Aaron Burr is born.

1772 Aaron Burr graduates college at age 16.

1782 Aaron Burr marries Theodosia Bartow Prevost.

1783 Aaron Burr's daughter Theodosia is born.

1791 Aaron Burr is elected to the US Senate.

1800 Aaron Burr becomes vice president of the United States.

1804 Aaron Burr duels with and kills Alexander Hamilton.

1807 Aaron Burr is arrested and charged with treason.

1813 Aaron Burr's daughter, Theodosia, disappears at sea.

1836 Aaron Burr dies of a stroke.

Hero or Villain?

Burr had a life filled with great highs and unbelievable lows. In some ways, he was a hero: he fought for the rights of immigrants, women, and poor people. In others, he was a villain: he may have made plans to overthrow the US government, and he killed Alexander Hamilton in a duel.

No one is all good or all bad, but Aaron Burr's silence about his own life hasn't helped anyone decide how to label him—and many of his letters were lost at sea with his daughter Theodosia.

Though we have many writings from the other Founding Fathers, few of Burr's letters and notes remain for us to study today.

Glossary

accuse: to blame someone for something

aide: someone whose job is to help a military officer

charter: a contract or document explaining the rights and duties of a group

debate: an argument or public talk about a certain topic

deport: to force a person to leave a country

duel: a fight with deadly weapons between two people, with witnesses present, because of a wrong done by one to the other

Electoral College: the body of specially chosen voters who represent the states and elect the US president

exile: the state of being away from one's country, often for a long period of time

House of Representatives: one part of Congress, which is the branch of US government that makes laws

immigrant: someone who comes to a country to settle there

propose: to suggest or make an offer

qualified: having the skills and experience needed to do an activity

traitor: a person who is not faithful to another person or group

undercover: acting in secret

For More Information

Books

Ingram, W. Scott. *Aaron Burr and the Young Nation*. Woodbridge, CT: Blackbirch Press, 2002.

Lucas, Eileen. *The Aaron Burr Treason Trial: A Headline Court Case*. Berkeley Heights, NJ: Enslow Publishers, 2003.

St. George, Judith. *The Duel: The Parallel Lives of Alexander Hamilton & Aaron Burr*. New York, NY: Viking, 2009.

Websites

Aaron Burr
pbs.org/wgbh/amex/duel/peopleevents/pande01.html
Learn all about the duel between Aaron Burr and Alexander Hamilton here.

Aaron Burr Association
aaronburrassociation.org
The Aaron Burr Association seeks to keep the memory of Aaron Burr alive with resources to learn about his life.

National Archives
archives.gov
See documents and materials from Burr's life here.

Publisher's note to educators and parents: Our editors have carefully reviewed these websites to ensure that they are suitable for students. Many websites change frequently, however, and we cannot guarantee that a site's future contents will continue to meet our high standards of quality and educational value. Be advised that students should be closely supervised whenever they access the Internet.

Index